D!ck Pic

First it's your secret, now it's ours.

Chapter 1

It was a pleasant drive home on a balmy evening as he maneuvered the streets with his white SUV. The twilight skies were ablaze with orange streaks and the traffic had slowly decongested. He whistled to an old Bee Gees song blaring from his car stereo.

His home, a five-storied castle, built in the orthodox style of royal mansions in the 80s, stood out in its immaculate white and overlooked a large piece of lawn. He usually felt his chest bloat with pride at the sight of it, just like his estate taking up a large stretch of land, with a string of well-furnished apartments, his inimitable, largely successful company, private jets and every other weighty accomplishment he had accrued over the years, all situated in the hearts of San Francisco. This time around, he didn't feel the usual excitement as he approached the house.

The moment he drove into his home he knew something was strange. His ears strained into the distance, the noises which emanated from inside sounded muffled; something was going on inside his mansion. *Had he been raided?* He wondered. He had fears of people wanting to tail him or rip him off his wealth like they did other wealthy men. He felt as though one could never have enough security, yet he hadn't done more than insert CCTV cameras in his home or anything else. He panicked. He could see through one of the windows, lights were going off and on upstairs. He turned off the car ignition, quickly got out of his car, and headed into the house. The noises, though stifled, came more alive as he drew closer to the second living room upstairs where it seemed the musical sounds vibrated from and he wondered what the hell was going on.

As he opened the door of the living room, the loud music exploded in his ears and the beat drummed heavily on his chest in quick rhythms; frenzied and deafening. The party was like some sort of inferno; hot and wild. The thick smell of marijuana and beer hit his nose. His eyes were almost bulging out of his socket moving through the dimly lit party where colored disco light flashed in patterns. Different forms of neon lights pierced into the darkness. Naked girls waved their glow sticks which came in different colors in the smoky air. He saw the lady bouncing herself on the laps of a young man, both of them stark naked, he figured that although they moved to the rhythm of the beat, they were not dancing at all, the man sat with a hard-on which was seven inches deep into his lap dancer. Others too, were naked, dancing with their clammy bodies too close. A fat lady was tubed in rubbery glow sticks that covered her womanly bits and she walked with very gentle steps so as not to let her costume disband from her body as she moved. A short guy was clad in a garbage bag, and it didn't take long to notice that the people who weren't stark naked were clad in different other things that weren't normal clothes. A guy made clanking sounds as he danced and the soda cans tied together and used in covering his nakedness jammed against each other.

The teenagers were overexcited and intoxicated, they slurred as they spoke and the ladies swayed their hips and danced provocatively to the loud music. Some men spilled champagne over the naked women and drank it off their sweaty skins. As the DJ saw him standing by the doorway, he whispered, "there's CEO of JC Corporation, Mr. James Carter, let me announce his presence with much dignity."

"Shhh... my dad doesn't like wild parties. He didn't know we were back home. we're in deep shit." Kevin said and rushed over to his dad.

"Uh oh, looks like the party's over." The DJ, who made a covering of his privates with discs stringed together, announced through his microphone. He lowered the music sound and everyone turned their attention to the stunned man standing by the doorway.

"Dad, you're h-home so s-soon." Kevin said to his dad in a panic.

James was totally speechless. "Kevin, what do you think you are doing? Look at my apartment, filled with all sizes of tits! What is this, an orgy party?"

"Dad, calm down...it's a reunion, a rehash of our college frat party, neon themed, and of course ABC." Kevin smiled proudly, feeling the panic gradually wear off the more they talked about it.

"And what in the world is ABC, you just left college and not preschool." he retorted.

"Oh, an ABC party simply means *Anything But Clothes*, as you can see. These guys are super creative but it appears we prefer those who didn't bother to use their creative juices at all." He cast a last glance towards the circle of naked ladies standing together and his grin went off his face when he saw how his dad's face flushed in anger.

"Are you nuts? Where the hell are your siblings, Richie and Rachael?"

"I'm surprised you haven't seen them, Richie is over there, with his friends smoking pot."

"Smoking what? When the hell did he pick up a habit of smoking?"

"He didn't dad, most college kids do it but they don't really smoke"

"Can you at least make sense...and where the hell is Rachael?" Kevin's eyes scanned the entire place while trying to catch a glimpse of his sister at the frantic party.

"Oh no, don't tell me my daughter is in here!"

"Over there, she's the one on a golden mask, lashing the man wearing a G-string with a long whip. She said she wanted to try out her new fetish, bad-o-sarcasm."

"It's sadomasochism." He slapped a hand over his forehead as though feeling stupid for having provided the correct word when he should remain mad at the whole thing. The party people were running helter-skelter, clearing up their paraphernalia, getting dressed, and putting away their drug pots, hard drinks, and condoms. Richie and Rachael came to stand with Kevin as they faced their dad whose frown had returned back to his face he breathed out to calm himself and then said to them "Now think. Think of how your late mom would have felt if she had walked in through that door as I did. She wouldn't even know her kids right now!"

"Dad, mom loved parties. She only subdued that side because of you all these years."

"Not this type of party at least."

"But dad, she liked the type for her age, and this party of ours is age appropriate. We've all just graduated from college dad." Rachael whined.

"Is inflicting pains on a naked man also age appropriate?" James rolled his eyes; he knew he would be getting into an argument with his kids, they knew that once the first minute of anger had gone by, he became soft and penetrable and they could get into his head with a simple argument. Sometimes he wondered if he was being a good parent alone, he felt that his being busy building his company gave a lot of freedom to the kids to explore way more than they should be doing, and this fact made him miss the joint effort of his wife in making sure they were on the right path. In the middle of his retrospection, he realized that the kids were still talking on and on.

"And YOLO dad! YOLO." Kevin was saying enthusiastically.

"And what the hell is that?"

"Oh dad, that's our little assignment for you," Rachael said boldly.

"Are you kidding? All dads know what YOLO is, only the stiff ones don't." Richie said teasingly.

"I will not continue with this conversation." He snapped "Now, you can throw your wild parties anywhere else but in my home ok? Once they have to take off their tops, take them away."

A smile came and went on Rachael's face.

"Understood dad."

"Fine."

"That's noted."

They all came to an agreement with him.

"Now that's better. No more YOLOS, whatever the hell that is." He said through gritted teeth and his kids stifled their laughter.

"It's bad enough that I have to deal with my crazy employees at work, now my children! What the hell is wrong with the world? Am I the only normal guy out there?"

Rachael went behind him to massage his shoulders briefly, "Daddy relax. Move with the pace, the world is only changing." She stopped and walked away, leaving them behind.

Mr. James Carter's wife Amanda was a slim petite woman with an aristocratic air which he greatly admired and thought befitting of his status. She adored him and did everything to please him, sometimes he wondered if she had also pleased herself or was she all about him. She had shown her wild side countable times and it often took him by surprise. He realized quickly that the children had taken after her and that perhaps it wasn't just societal nurture that had groomed his kids into their level of craziness, perhaps it was also a part of their nature which they had adopted from their mother unconsciously. She sometimes wore G-strings and stayed in provocative positions she had seen in some adult magazines, but that happened once in a blue moon when they were alone. He had also heard her talk dirty to him in bed and he was taken aback, first she called him a tiger, and then she spanked his butt when she got carried away with pleasure and screamed "dig my hole, you naughty handyman." He had asked her what she meant by "handyman" and she simply admitted that she role-played in her head.

"For a moment, I was the horny and lonely housewife who had called in the plumber to check on my leaky faucet, and then I became the leaky faucet and you, the plumber, worked on me and drained me." She stopped to look at him for a moment, to weigh the impact of her provocativeness on him, hoping she hadn't offended him with it.

"Oh my God, who are you?" James blushed heavily, not sure how else to react. "Well, we both enjoyed it at least." He finally said, "But next time, I will not stoop from being a billionaire to a common plumber screwing some cuckolding housewife."

They both laughed.

Other times she had remained calm, gentle, and moderate in bed, following his lead obediently and he felt very comfortable. One night again she suddenly screamed in the middle of an orgasm "harder you horny blue whale."

Minutes after the sex, James had asked "Is my size just right for you? I don't know...A blue whale has the largest penis in the world. Why would you think of that?"

"Oh no, it's not about the size of the penis, it's about the heart, it has a very big heart, it weighs around 180kg, that's roughly 400 pounds."

"No shit, for its enormous size what were we to expect?"

"It figuratively means kindness and generosity for me. You are the sweetest man in the world James."

"I'm flattered darling but if you say I'm a blue whale, here's a fun fact; it has a relatively small brain too, just 7kg, which is 15 pounds, only 0.007 percent of its entire body weight."

A smile came and went on her face, "Have we been reading the same book?"

"Smarty pants," he said and began to nuzzle on her neck while she laughed out.

From time to time, his kids held parties, some at home, some away from home and they had gone from subtle college parties with the potential of getting high and getting laid at the end of the party to downright crazy orgy parties where they did what their dad would describe as abominable. They however had been caught for the first time and had decided to tone it down. Their idea of toning it down was to have more decent parties at home and take the wild parties to other locations.

The ostrich park, a place Amanda loved to spend time the most, flashed into James's memory. He played Bee Gees as usual in his car, at a moderate volume as they drove home after a dinner date. His wife, who had taken an extra glass of wine more than she usually does had raised the volume and sang along with one of the hit songs of the band; *staying alive*.

"Turn it down sweetheart. I don't like loud music in the car. It reminds me of college kids."

"Darling, this is a great time to be carefree for once."

"Wait a minute, you don't have your seat belt on?"

"There's no..." her voice trailed off and she quickly fumbled for her seat belt and while she did, he lowered the volume. After she had worn her seat belt, she looked at him and forced a little smile. He thought of that smile, it was a bit of a sad one, he had prided himself on being able to read her but not this time around. Later he would remember why she wanted the music so loud, why she suddenly wanted to be carefree and why she hadn't bothered to wear her seat belt which she barely forgot.

He would remember how her smile had turned sad as though she was disappointed in him at the moment or there was a secret in her heart which he would later figure out.

He sat in the living room, his apple laptop in front of him as he looked up the word YOLO which his children had assigned him to figure out – it read, *you only live once*. He breathed out gloomily.

Amanda's cervical cancer was far gone before she finally opened up to him about it. "I didn't want you to get distraught darling." She said to him on her sick bed with her three children by her side. "You need to be emotionally fit to run the company you've built for many years. I only wanted a few extra days to live carefree, without restraints."

Wanting the volume turned up while her favorite song played in the car stereo was the simplest wish a patrician woman like Amanda could make to him in her last days on earth. The sad smile he had observed on her face lingered from time to time. She had put him and his company first before herself, she had thought of his wellbeing and had chosen to die in silence because the next few days after they had driven home from that park after he had failed to turn up the volume of the car stereo after she had forced a smile and left him a disturbing note, Amanda died at the hospital bed.

He could feel the lump in his throat; emotions overwhelmed him for the second time in his life, the first had been the moment he found out about her terminal illness. He shut down his laptop and went to sleep, clutching onto Amanda's most worn nightie; a lilac satin nightgown that still smelled faintly of her lily flower scent. In the next minute, the room was filled with the sounds of his snoring and the curtains flailed gently to the night breeze.

Chapter 2

James Carter's office was in the hearts of San Fransisco; a huge 15-story glass office surrounded by gardens and several other skyscrapers. He had labored to establish the company which majored in big-time advertising, marketing, and publicity, running their in-house media which is affiliated with the major media outlets in town. Other sublets of the company were a printing press and an entrepreneurial school. He had employees which he had personally interviewed before employing, as there were special characteristics he wanted in his workforce, little did he know that since he chose to employ men and women who had skills in activism, who were extremely creative and bold, he would have an office full of crazy.

There was Carlos, a gay activist who for a moment had struck James as a carbon copy of himself. As the interview with Carlos started he looked at him carefully, his face, the shape of his hair and chin, and his eyes and lips looked almost identical to his.

"You catch my interest." James said to Carlos and it was obvious to the both of them what he meant, Carlos said to him "And you too sir."

James looked down at his profile and saw the letters boldly written: *public speaker and gay activist.*

“Not in that crazy way Carlos.” He quickly chipped in, not sure what was on Carlos’s mind.

“I wish I knew in what way you speak of.” he smiled and winked at James who turned his face down to the files again and pretended not to notice Carlos's flirtatiousness. He made up his mind that if Carlos did not have the level of intellectual ability he wanted, regardless of their resemblance or whatever was written on his profile, he wouldn’t hire him, but during the interview, the oral and written test, Carlos wowed James.

“Brilliant.” James admitted from across the table, “You have the job.” He said and moved forward to shake Carlos who also extended his hand, and as soon as he took James’s hands in his, he scratched on the palm with his index finger flirtatiously and goose pimples ran through James’s body.

The other employees didn’t also fall short of the impression he was looking for, there was Delilah, a busty Latina lady with a good sense of humour who used to work in a strip club as a stripper.

“Why do you want this job?” James asked Delilah during their interview.

“I’m sure you’ve seen my profile sir. I don’t have the best of job experiences but I’m honest enough to put it out. I’m good at maths.”

“Your records say so, the written tests too. Go on please”

"I studied accounting but haven't been able to get a good accounting job. I believe my degree in accountant will handle the professional bit and my honesty which is needed in the finance department will handle the moral bit."

"Well, this should permanently keep you off the strip bars or wherever it is you go to tease men, you have it here now."

Delilah had a sly twinkle in her eyes, he noticed it and quickly chipped in "Oh no, I'm not saying you should bring it in here, I'm sure you know what I mean." He laughed a little.

"Yes of course James. I know exactly what you mean."

He moved his toe underneath the table in a gentle retreat from hers before realizing that she hadn't toes teased him and it was all in his head. *You watch too many movies* he thought to himself. Delilah retreated her toes too, smart guy, he knew just what I was about to do, and their eyes locked a bit before he got up quickly. "So you have it, you will resume with us..."

"Tomorrow?"

"That's alright Delilah."

There was Reeves, a man who had made substantial wins from Wall Street. He was adept at financial investments and digital assets, he however played heavy poker and had the most erratic net worth in history; he was rich in a week and near broke the next. He was carefree and took life with a pinch of salt, he needed some sort of stability in his finances so he applied for a job at JC Corporation, and perhaps he could live a normal life again. While James would have written him off as a degenerate gambler, he however had enormous experience and exposure to stocks, bonds and other digital assets which James believed would serve as a separate investment sector for his company, so Reeves got the job.

There was also Nicky, the financial advisor who managed the entrepreneurial training subdivision of his company and Fred who simply just graduated from Harvard and looked young and with a lot of potentials for JC incorporation to harness.

The following morning Delilah had resumed work "Good morning James, you look smart in that suit."

"It's Carlos, my name is Carlos Estefan."

Delilah was taken aback, "Oh my word, of course Carlos, apologies. Did anyone ever tell you that you look like our boss?"

"And sound like him too." a voice boomed out from behind, it was Tyler. They turned to look at Tyler, a dark skinned man on glasses. "Hi guys, I'm the personal assistant to James."

They shook hands and had a brief onboarding meeting at the conference room.

"We will meet here every Monday morning and also have an end of the month meeting on the last Friday of the month." James addressed them briefly.

During lunch break the staff had lunch together at the cafeteria down the building and talked causally.

“So Tyler, I noticed the easy rapport between you and James” Delilah said.

“Yeah, we actually shared friendship before I got employed here. We went to the same college, he found me online and asked me to come become his personal assistant, he knew how much competence I would bring, but of course, he needed a man who already understands him and can fit into this position and play his role at any time.”

Carlos looked at him enviously and said “I obviously wouldn’t have fitted into that position of yours.”

“Oh yeah, people wouldn’t know the difference between you and him when you go out to meet with important clients.”

“Yes and that too.” Carlos said, thinking about how it would have been a distraction for him to work so closely with James who he was already sexually attracted to, he smiled at his secret thoughts.

“He is actually a very nice man, you would all enjoy working here, however, that man don’t play. You gotta get serious when he needs you to be serious. He’s very result oriented and I believe many of us can meet up, I actually went through the staff profiles.”

“Are you kidding me?” Delilah said “So you know who I was right?”

"Seeing is believing." Tyler said and winked, "I'll find out at the weekend's onboarding dinner party, if you don't mind giving us a little private show."

"There's an onboarding party?"

"Shhh...it's unofficial. We will be having these special events once in a while, just to unwind. James has made provisions, he appears to listen to my suggestions quite a lot. I'm in the position to ensure that everything is working just fine, but you all must work hard and take this company to its heights."

"That's totally great" Delilah said, her Latina accent pushing through her words.

"I look forward to the dinner party" Young Fred said.

Reeves and Selena exchanged smiles.

"He really is a nice man." Carlos said, and began growing a boner in his pants as he thought of James, what he didn't know was that his auto-sexuality extends beyond being sexually attracted to his own self, he was completely into his mirror image and had immediate sexual attraction towards men with attributes like himself. He often thought about how much his homosexuality came with a little twist since he enjoyed masturbation than getting involved with others, especially those who didn't look like him. Delilah who sat next to him noticed his hard on almost as quickly as it had appeared, she was very quick and observant. “Release the tension.” She whispered. Carlos smiled shyly and said, “Don’t worry about it.”

The onboarding dinner party was a success, the dinner party hall was filled with elegantly dressed staff and guest and James sat and watched them dance. Carlos cracked jokes around his CEO and flirted with him from time to time and he carefully evaded his advances. “I like our CEO, he’s really reserved and a little geeky, Carlos said to Reeves who listened while downing shots after shots of tequila. “Do you know I bumped into him at the gents and I think he zipped too quickly when he saw me. I know this ‘cause he let out a little yelp, I think he must have zipped a sac”

Reeves almost choked on his tequila “What if you had only startled him. Besides, why do you pay attention to these things Carlos?” Reeves asked with a raised brow.

“I’m just a little bit sensitive.” He smiled.

Delilah danced wildly. She brushed her behind on them intentionally and whispered into the ears of the men in a seductive voice. Nicky thought she was being awkward, but apparently, the men enjoyed her presence all the way. As soon as Nicky noticed how it worked, she began to draw closer to Delilah so she could take part in all the attention she got from men as well.

“She’s a big teaser” Tyler said excitedly, she danced with the CEO and I could have sworn he hasn’t gotten a hold of himself ever since. Carlos rolled his eyes.

The onboarding party went by and the staffs began to bond and build JC Corporation into something that James hadn’t previously imagined. He worked as much as they did and spent his leisure hours at home on his system, looking for better ideas for his company and bringing those ideas to life through his active staff. His kids thought he was too serious and worked too much. In the next couple of years JC Corporation became a well-known empire in san Fransisco. James wished that his wife was alive to see how successfully the company was thriving. He missed her a lot. Once in a while he looked through her things in the wardrobe, unwilling to put them away, he sniffed and cuddled them as though Amanda had left a part of her inside of those things.

That morning he was staring at her favourite G-string, he was dressing up for work and he felt a little empty on the inside. All that success with the deep loneliness he felt was enough to drive him crazy on some days. In the next hour he was on his way to work, a little earlier than usual. It was barely 7:30am in the morning.

James realized he had come to work earlier than everyone else as he sometimes does. He went to the conference room, sat down and picked up a magazine on the table. It was a feminine magazine with all sorts of sensual contents and images inside its pages. He thought that it must obviously belong to Delilah and he thought to himself, you can take a woman out of the country but you can never take the country out of the woman. An involuntary smile appeared on his face. There was a at the mid cover she glance at the page in full and she had Amanda's bright blue eyes, a thought struck him, he remembered the G-string he had picked up from her closet in the morning, he had slid into it and just as he thought of it, he could feel the string buried deep in his bum crack, he flushed a little bit; this was probably one of the craziest things he's ever done so far – wearing his wife's G-string to work, just to satiate himself of the longing for her.

As soon as he slid his hand into his trousers to adjust the string part that uncomfortably went deep between his butts, he noticed how hard he had become and the feminine wear was finding it hard to hold his turbidity. "Fuck it" he muttered and pushed the G-string away from his hard cock, freeing it for a moment. The model in the magazine stared deep into his eyes or so it appeared, he let out a soft groan and began to tug at his trouser, pulling it off entirely.

"Oh fuck me." He muttered. He rubbed on his cap gently, it was warm and in dire need of a woman's vagina. He stroked his shaft all the way down and up and down again, he threw his head back and moaned while thrusting gently into his soft sweaty palms. "Amanda" he whispered and then he began to thrust a little quicker and harder, unable to hold back at this point, he was in a full jerk off mode when a loud bang suddenly happened and he watched the door of the meeting room swinging ajar and the little chatter of the staff gave him an awakening. His heart skipped several beats, his cheeks flushed red and he quickly took his hand off his hard cock which poked out of the G-string he was wearing, he grabbed onto his trouser, feeling glad that he was at least covered by the conference table and no one could see that he was naked underneath and no one could possibly suspect since he wore a neat black suit and a white shirt on top.

"Good morning Mr. Carter." His staff greeted in unison. He panicked as he watched them all troop in, his stomach churned uncomfortably; this had to be the worst day of his life yet.

"Ah...Good morning guys...I...I was a tad earlier than usual so I decided to s-sit here for a while and read a little fun stuff." He laughed nervously.

"We thought you were just right on time for our meeting." Reeves said

"What, what meeting? We have a meeting?"

"Sure sir, our end of the month meeting remember?" Delilah said

"Oh, yes, yes, I have so much on my mind I totally forgot." His nervous little laugh came briefly again.

They all took a seat and the meeting began immediately with Tyler briefing them on the plans they had outlined for the coming month. James couldn't contribute much, he appeared to agree with everything they suggest as he was restless and conscious of what he looked like underneath the table. Delilah was seated a few metres away from him, she was stirring up applauds for Tyler's points and apparently engrossed in his presentation.

"And then we will move in with our plan and seal the deal." Tyler was saying.

Delilah started up another applaud, unfortunately, her pen dropped from her clumsy clapping. James whispers "God please!" as Delilah bends and picks up her pen. She goes mute and suddenly straight faced for a second. With shoulders squared and chin up, she started saying "Hey boss, you know what? This is the perfect time to give me a salary raise isn't it?"

James could feel his heart almost leaping out of his chest "W-What?"

"We discussed this before. I need my raise now."

Bouts of cough erupted from him, he felt obviously sabotaged, there was no way out for him at that moment. *Bitch*, he thought and rubbed the sudden throbbing temples of his head. He didn't want the conversation to prolong; it was the surest way of avoiding all further curiosities of the other staff. "Yes, yes, You...you have it Delilah. I'm giving you a raise." The other staff half astonished and half envious immediately began to congratulate Delilah.

"Woohoo!"

"You go girl!"

"You deserve it!"

"All your hard work has finally paid off."

Delilah smiled, wet her lips with her tongue and started to say immediately "And oh boss, my girl Nicky is not at work today, she also needs a raise boss."

A dreadful silence sweeps across the meeting room.

James felt his face drain of colour. "Whoa, I er...well..." he laughed nervously again and said right after weighing his options and what's at stake "Yes, she got it. I'm also giving her a raise! I'll put it in paper as well." he said through gritted teeth such that it was quite noticeable that he had given the raise rather grudgingly.

The other staff stared at each other in confusion, wondering what's going on, their eyes were silently inquisitive but they couldn't question the CEO's rights to giving incentives for individual efforts, expressed nothing more than high-spirited congratulations to Delilah and Nicky. In the next thirty minutes, the meeting was over and the staff left the meeting room in a single file. Delilah was the last in to leave, before she left, she bent over to whispers to James in her mellifluous Latina accent "You need to get a girlfriend fast before you ruin your career Papi."

Chapter 3

The morning unraveled slowly, lighting up the white castle home and the streets gradually began to fill with cars and people. James had convinced himself that it was high time he found a woman, same way he had convinced himself that it had nothing to do with Delilah's words or the little incident at the meeting room.

They can't possibly dictate to me when I want a partner, he said stubbornly, but clicked away on the various profiles of the single women on dating sites. He had thought about the fastest way to get hooked up, he knew that the probability might be higher looking through dating sites than going out to talk to women individually, on dating sites it was like being handed a menu book in a restaurant where everything was there at once and all he needed do was glance through and make a pick or two.

He wondered that the idea never came to him mind all along, he was still thinking a lot about Amanda, but he was growing lonelier by the day. He was looking through the various women profiles on dating sites when his son Kevin walked into his room.

"At what point does this become desperate?" he said to him, "I mean, looking through dating sites by this time, is that even okay?"

"This is the famous guilt trip dad. It is very okay, this is the modern way of hooking up, you've been long overdue to find a partner, and it's not desperate at all. We all want you to move on. Don't think we do not notice the things you do around the house."

"What do I do?" he stopped to look at him, wondering what he was talking about.

"You make use of mom's G-strings and all that creepy shit."

James cringed and changed the topic quickly. "What are the best dating sites these days? I'm not even sure I'm checking the right ones."

"Why do you say so?"

"Just look at their pictures, they're far too provocative. Look at that! She's almost naked, you mom would never wear that!" he gestured towards the screen.

"Dad, everyone isn't the same, if you ever want to move on, don't compare." he drew closer to look at the picture "Dad, she's got huge tits, what's your idea of perfection these days?" he rolled his eyes, "FYI I would like to know the name of this dating site."

"What do you need that for Kevin?"

"Dad I'm not a kid."

"You need to grow up decently."

Kevin wasn't paying attention, he was typing the website name into his phone keypad.

"You're not being helpful Kevin."

"Dad, you keep forgetting we're all grown-ups, this isn't the 60s"

"You kids sound like a broken record when you keep reminding me how grown up you are whenever you are doing something horrible."

When James was finally left alone, he began to dial the numbers of the few women he had found attractive one after the other.

"Hello, I'm I speaking with Ann?" he said, feeling a little tensed at doing something he's never done before.

"Yes, this is Ann speaking, Ann Al"

"Ann Al?"

"Yes cowboy, I'm sorry my name sounds that way. My surname was cox just before papa disowned me for turning a stripper and my full name was Anita, but men used to tease me a lot with that."

"Anita Cox?"

"Yesss." She said in a sensual tone.

"I think I might have dialed the wrong number." James hung up the phone. he thought that was the most awkward conversation he's ever had with a stranger.

He called a few others and changed his mind about meeting them. He didn't know if it had to do with his mental readiness or the way the women sounded too forward. He looked through his inbox and some other lady had replied to his message.

As they talked further, he steeled his mind this time around and arranged for them to meet. As the date went on, it became like some sort of interview. He needed to know more about her since she wasn't asking deep questions about him asides what brand of wristwatch that was on his wrist and how he had picked out the cologne he was wearing.

"What kind of a man do you like?" he began.

"Stinking rich plus a lot older."

"Any particular reasons?"

"There ought to be some sort of retirement benefits from being with an old man don't you think?"

James froze, it was the most cringe-worthy thing he had ever been told. "If it's such hard work, why not go for younger guys?"

"They don't have the kind of money I'm looking for."

"You will find what you're looking for and thanks for your honesty, I wish you goodluck."

"I found him already" she said with a wink and squeezed his thigh with her hand.

“I’m not the guy for you.”

“Ok then, is there anything we could do on a quicker time frame?”

“Nothing at all.”

She seemed taken aback as though this particular man had fallen down from space, she hadn’t encountered his type before, and no man ever passes on an opportunity to lay with her.

“You aren’t horny?”

“As a matter of fact, I’m hungry and tried. So I’ll just finish up with my lamb chop and head home for a nap.”

The date was over.

He decided not to give up just yet. He met several other women from dating sites, went on a date with them and tried to figure them out. They either sounded too wild for his taste or they were gold-diggers. One directly spoke of getting married to him, if only some of his properties would be willed to her. He froze on his food and lost his appetite.

Soon the women from the dating sites began to text him a lot and send nude pictures and videos of them using sex toys on themselves. Betty, the one he admired but didn’t want to have anything serious with was bombarding his phone with calls and messages. “I have something you’re going to like James” she said and immediately his phone bleeped, she had sent him a sexy video. “Take a look at that and tell me I’m not a keeper.” She said proudly.

When James opened the short clip she saw Betty inserting a big black dildo into her vagina, it was as real looking as possible, extra-large, a shiny plastic black with a long vein running across its shaft. She moaned as the dick went into her and out and then she brought it out, shiny and slick with her fluids and began to suck on the cap and run her tongue over the vein on the shaft.

“Oh my God.” James said and flushed, he quickly deleted the short clip, wondering why she would be so attracted to an extra-large size with a fetish for the vein running over the plastic black dick. He began to think that it may be petty that he wondered why she would have her particular taste, perhaps it was just that the that dick is almost the opposite of his, which suggested to him that she accommodated a wide range but what he had found disturbing was that he had kind of felt like the dildo would be a lot of trouble going into her for its enormous size, but it had vanished inside of her at the slightest single push.

He remembers that she was still expecting a response from him and he quickly typed and sent his last message to her. “I’m overwhelmed.”

The last couple of weeks were rather slow for him. He greatly admired Tyler’s ability to handle the office without him. Soon he began to let him in on his search for a partner and he was amazed at how Tyler seemed knowledgeable and wise about different areas of life, including dating and women. He always had an advice, a suggestion and most of the time, it left him amazed and impressed.

“They are still decent women on dating sites, try out a few more, read subtle signs, you need a soul mate for stability.” Tyler urged him.

“What’s going on at the office?”

“Just work and a little chitchat, and hey, Carlos is missing you.”

James scoffed. He got off the phone with Tyler, feeling a little energized, and he decided to give online dating sites a final chance, this time around he may stumble across Mrs. Right.

Chapter 4

The bell rang, James groggily stood up, he hated it when the kids weren't home, He gets to get the door himself. As soon as he peeked through the door lens, he saw a familiar face; one of the women he had recently met online had decided to pay him and unannounced visit. He opened the door.

"Gwendolyn!"

"That's right, I told you to keep it simple, Gwen's better."

"If you were a woman of simplicity, you would have told me you would be coming"

"I like spontaneous, just like I assume everyone else does."

James rolled his eyes.

She walked into the house, her eyes wandering in awe at the beauty of James's home. "I love this place. It's going to be awesome to have and raise my kids here."

"That's if I decide to sell it to you or your future spouse."

James chipped in.

"You're a funny man, I like humour" her voice had become a flirtatious tone.

"What would you like to have?"

"Hard chili martini or chocolate rye."

I don't have any of those aphrodisiacs.

"Then I'll have whatever you're having.

"Just a glass of milk...and donuts"

She rolled her eyes. He seemed to be deliberately thwarting her efforts.

They sat watching a comedy TV show. "Isn't there some romantic movie to see?"

"Here," he handed her the remote control "feel free to scan the channels."

"Sometimes I like soggy donuts, ever tried it inside milk?" she said

"How do I achieve that, do I dip it in?" James asked

She bit her lower lip. "I like the sound of that, you can dip it in, push it, pump it, roll it."

"We're talking about the donuts right?"

"Oh, yes, you can also do that with the donut."

He seemed to have lost his appetite.

"Oh, I found the perfect channel for us" she said

"That's fine, but could you turn it down, it's a little loud."

"Loud is good baby, don't you like it? I can be pretty loud at it, I like that the kids aren't home." she began to kiss and lick his face, unbuttoning his trousers at the same time.

"For goodness sakes, Gwendolyn."

"She bit on his lower lip."

"Ouch!"

"Hush, you naughty boy" she closed his mouth on his and kissed him deeply. He began to push his way off her pressing body and roving hands. He wondered if he had locked the door and what if the kids came in. he didn't want to be seen that way, at least not with Gwendolyn. He pulled away from her.

"What are you doing Gwen?"

She lunged at him and he fell over the rug, she pulled up her dress and sat on him in his half fallen trouser. She slipped her hand into his trouser and brought out his limp cock, "Now let's have this little man up."

"Stop it Gwen"

She spat on it.

"What the hell!"

She began to stroke it. "It's so hot and big when it's up." She moaned.

"Just stop!" he seemed embarrassed that his dick had responded to her touch.

She stroked harder with a hand and pulled her panties aside and sat gently over his rigid cock. Just when he felt his cap sliding into her cunt, he gave her a hard push which shoved her to the ground.

"That's it, you cannot come into my home and sexually assault me Gwen, you shall take your leave now!"

"But it was just a..."

"Now!" he got to his feet and opened the door for her.

Let me touch up on my dress and make up she said in an angry tone. She took five minutes to refresh her make up and left James's apartment.

He breathed out, wondering what sort of women are out there. He knew that it was partially because he was rich, but looking into the mirror he wasn't bad looking either. They all failed to understand the needs of an orthodox man as he. For people like him the progression was simple and modest; you meet a lady, fall in love, woo her and she agrees if she likes you, then along the line, sex happens. But these days, he wondered that it happens the other way round; have sex, then she agrees to date you if she enjoyed it, then you guys go ahead and fall in love and then you meet her, the real her. James thought that the world was gradually turning upside down and he will never understand the next generation, they cared too much for pleasure, they liked riches but they enjoyed a lifestyle that was the exact opposite lifestyle of those who make genuine lasting wealth. He wondered if he was raising his kids up to be just like the dreaded generation, somehow, he's got them financially covered so he knew he needn't worry much.

In the next few minutes his kids came back, he felt glad that he had dismissed Gwen just before they did. Richie's nose was upturned, "I smell something."

"Yes, me too" Rachael said.

"Yes, I...someone..." James fumbled for what to say

"Like donuts."

"Oh that! Yes, I had donuts."

"Someone paid you a visit right?"

"Yes, that's also true."

"A woman?"

"Oh my God, tell us about her dad. You hardly have them visit!"

"You should have let her stay back so she could meet us."

"No! It's not that kind of visitor and no, she's not the type I would want my kids to meet"

"Was she a one night stand?"

"Kevin, stop. It's not that way, you know me too well"

"But that's the problem dad, you need company, you don't want to die a lonely man, do you?"

"I won't"

"Fine, so then find someone."

The next day, James visited the office, the staffs were glad to see him. Carlos asked him out on a date which he immediately declined. Tyler filled him in on everything that's being going on, including the progress and financial growth of the company. James was extremely proud of their efforts. The moment he got home, his kids who had been discussing something decided to let him into their discussion.

"Dad, tomorrow is your birthday" Kevin said

James was taken aback "Oh, That's right boy. I seem to have a head full of office plans and activities that I almost forgot about that"

"So, Rachael, Richie and I came up with something." Kevin continued

"Anything that isn't crazy is acceptable."

"It depends...because since we want you to find someone, we decided to throw a big birthday party for you. All arrangements are ongoing."

“Kevin, that could have been better as a surprise don’t you think?” Rachael said.

“No, because he is supposed to know what to expect and what we expect of him.”

“And what would that be?”

“Dad, you’re going to enjoy life with a younger girl. So we thought of hooking you up with any of our female friends at your birthday party.”

James wore a straight face. “You want to hook me up with a college chic?”

“Exactly. You need a young lady who would revive your old bones.”

“First of all, don’t make me look older than I actually am, secondly, I don’t think it would work.”

“Why dad?”

“Our thought sand ideologies would be so far apart. The only thing that’s going to be on her mind would be parties and shopping sprees, she wouldn’t be capable of being a real partner whom I can make life decisions with or seek an advice from. Girls that age are still grappling their way around life, they wouldn’t make a good partner for me.”

“Dad, times have changed, younger people are a lot smarter and exposed than you can ever imagine, but you wouldn’t know if you don’t let them in would you?”

"Wouldn't they have a problem with being with an older man?"

"Very thoughtful of you dad, but these set of girl, they seem to like older men."

"That's a good thing right, I'm not very sure." James said.

"It's a good thing for you dad, that's all that matters." Rachael assured.

Half-heartedly James decided to go with his children's advice. He was more excited about the party itself. He called up Tyler "Tomorrow's my birthday, party's at my house."

"Damn, we're already trying to surprise you with one over here at the office. Shhh, it's still a secret, for the rest"

"Wow. That's very thoughtful of you guys. I'm going to have to split myself into two."

"Or have Carlos attend the one at your home, you know, impersonate you."

He laughed out "My kids will rope him out of homosexuality. They're that scheming"

They laughed.

"Ok, here's the deal, I'll be with the office in the morning till noon and then I'll be home with the kids for an extension which you are all invited."

"Perfect."

Chapter 5

The following day James was awoken by his kids, all three of them singing in keyless tones, waving their hands in the air like chief choristers.

“Happy birthday to you...” they sang.

James got up on his pajamas, watching his kids with a big smile on his face, as soon as they finished singing they threw themselves at him and they all hugged.

“Today’s a really special day dad.”

“We got you this.” Rachael couldn’t wait for a prolonged speech in order to present their birthday gift to him. James watched her bring it forward, it was wrapped in a shiny gift wrapper, he tore it open and revealed the box. He opened the box and there was a phone in it.

“Wow, a brand new phone!” he said, feeling happy that they had tried to impress him at all. “Where’s the power button?”

“Over here dad” Richie helped turn it on for him.

“Wow, It’s really cool and sophisticated.” He said, I happen to stay in my little bubble, keeping away from these latest gadgets ‘cause it would require some learning and getting used to.

"We know dad, you're used to these simpler ones in your possession, which by the way, the world is shifting from."

"Yeah dad, move with the pace." They sniggered at him, and watch him punch his fingers on the screen. He suddenly raised up the phone to his face and smiled "cheese" he said.

"Dad, no one says that when taking pictures anymore."

They waited a while.

"Let's have a look, they peeped at the picture he was taking and realized he hadn't taken a picture, he was recording instead.

"Dad, you really have to get used to this honestly, that's a friggin' video clip you did, not a photo. Now give it to Kevin and he'll take you a nice birthday morning shot on your PJs."

He laughed and then posed for Kevin's shot.

They looked at it.

"Wow, it's so spic and clear."

"For what it cost, it should be" Kevin said.

"Ok guys, while you do what you have to do for the house party, I'll be on my way to the office, my staff... they are expecting me."

In the next few hours, the party planner had transformed the living room space and there was soft music in the background. The caterers brought in all sorts of dishes and the dinning set was fillet with a buffet of assortments. Cocktail drinks, wine and champagne were lined up and the guests were slowly arriving.

James got to his office on time and the lights were all out, as soon as he stepped in, he strained his eyes in the dark “Where’s the party.”

“Oh fuck!” a voice called out

“It was meant to be a surprise, who told him?’”

The lights came on and James saw the already arranged venue. Balloons and ribbons with cardboard paper writings which spelled out his name in full and wished him a happy birthday.

“Come on guys, I’m a little psychic. I kinda knew you guys will be up to this.”

They all knew it was a lie and they began nudging, and punching at Tyler who just laughed and evaded their playful punches.

He stayed at the office, took a few cocktail with them, danced with Delilah and Carlos. Gave them a warm speech of gratitude and encouragement and in the next hour he was on his way back home while they turned the office party into some provocative strip party, feeling glad that James wasn’t there after all. The ladies were on sexy underwear, some lacey some very light and the men taken off their clothes and wore just singlet and briefs, Tyler had excitedly stripped down to his briefs alone.

They danced wildly and dry humped each other. Carlos watched reeves dance alone and got a hard on, he left into the gents and began to jerk off his hard cock and in a few minutes he groaned and made a mess of himself. Tyler danced with Delilah in a quiet selection of the office, so close that her lap dance became a sexual torment on his throbbing erection. "If I wrote you a cheque right now, would you slip it in for a minute?" his voice was raspy and desperate.

"Yes, if you don't nut all over me" she replied, and as quickly as she had spoken he had freed his hard cock from his brief. "Shut the door."

Back at James's apartment, the birthday party was buzzing. The college girls whom his kids had invited were young, nubile and charming. James danced around with them, had small conversations and tried to weigh their level of intelligence and understanding of life. He was getting amused at various points of their conversation.

Kevin pulled him aside "How's it going dad?"

"I wouldn't say it's going as planned but I'm at least having fun."

"That's not totally bad."

James found it a little absurd that a college girl, Chloe, had groped him in the kitchen. "I want the hot dog," she said and he moved away from the kitchen island where the pack of hotdog lay. "Nice one daddy" she said in a raspy voice, I mean yours"

“What?” before he could understand what she was up to, she grabbed his crotch and he jumped “Oh no, not that, you can’t do that Chloe.”

“I can do whatever I want, I was told you wanted a young girl. I’m here for you.”

In the midst of his growing erection and the way Chloe brushed her body against his, he managed to push his way out of her prowling hands and out of the kitchen, breathing hard.

While another, Henrietta had followed him up to his bedroom, as he changed his loafers for something more comfortable, he felt the door open behind him and Henrietta was right there walking up to him. “Hi, I was just about to...” her mouth closed against his in a deep kiss, he was in a state of confusion for a moment and he kissed back impulsively, her lips were soft and tasted of cherry.

“Your bed is king size, it’s pretty.’

“Yes, and off limits”

“Come on, I saw the way you stared at me”

“It was just an innocent...” her lips closed on his again and she placed his palm on her cleavage and moaned into his ears, but this time around he got a grip of himself and stepped back from her.

“The party’s waiting”

“So am I”

He nicely requested that they go back to the party and he made sure that he never made eye contact with any of the girls for not more than two seconds.

“Dad, who’s on your radar?” Rachel came over to ask him.

“Jesus, it seems these college girls are all cougars, where the hell did you get them from. I’m sure you’re not like that honey.” Before he could complete his statement, the picture of his daughter whipping the half-naked guy at the crazy party the other day crossed his mind, he sighed.

“Dad, we just wanna know if you’ve finally seen anyone” she said rolling her eyes at every other thing he had just said.

“I feel as though you all are tailing me, it’s a little worrisome but I think things will fall into place when we least expect.

“Dad, what does that even mean? You know, I ask this question because my friend Sarah is really into you.”

“Oh, is that so?”

“Yes dad, over there, she’s open for a conversation or so.”

She left him behind. James thought that the best way to stay off having too many of these encounters was to focus on a girl and a recommended one at that might just be the best option, so he sidled up to Sarah for a talk.

“Having fun?” he started

"Sure, I was looking for an indication of your age, some write it bluntly over the decoration, some use the number of balloons."

"Oh, so did you count the balloons on that stage."

"You bet."

James smiled. They chatted about several other things, about Rachel, Kevin and Richie, about college and then about each other.

"He's been talking for a while with her now, think it's going smooth?" Richie said to Rachael.

"I suppose. I can see she's free with him. I never even knew she drank, that's a glass of tequila in her hands."

"I think she's really cool." Kevin said.

The party went on till late in the evening. James excused himself from Sarah, they had become the centre of attraction, all the other girls looked at them enviously, and they wished he had picked them instead. He went over to his kids and whispered "Thanks guys for this awesome party and Rachael, I think Sarah's very interesting, she can hold really great conversation, so far it's going so well. I can't wait to know other things about her."

Rachael threw a victorious fist in the air. Kevin said "Finally!"

"And oh, it's getting pretty late, we should wrap up the party and I should give Sarah a drive home."

"Sounds good buddy" Kevin said. In the next few minutes the party people began to disperse. James drove Sarah his car. "I really had fun with you today, you're a great conversationalist and you're funny"

"Thanks James. But I don't think you really had the ideal fun."

They were speeding through the express. She continued talking while he was curiously attentive.

"While we spent time together at the party, I noticed you aren't so flexible."

"What do you mean?"

"You're a little rigid, and I'm afraid, slightly boring, you could do try a little excitement here and there"

"Oh!" he exclaimed and feigned a little laugh "I appreciate your being blunt if that's what you really feel, but it's not a kind of feedback that's new to me. People always say that to me but actually fun doesn't build mega companies, and exciting is for employees."

"I saw the way you behaved when I tried to massage you, you seemed tired from today. Parties can be exciting, you seemed overwhelmed by yours."

"You tried to massage me...in public Sarah"

"Oh was that the problem? I don't know how many guys would think that even matters. We weren't even naked."

For a few minutes they drove quietly. “So what do you think about me?” Sarah asked.

“I told you, you have a good sense of humour and you could hold really interesting conversations, I had fun talking with you today”

Sarah breathed out gently, as though she expected to hear something else, it was a party and she had expected him to do the things she would expect from a guy during their college parties but he was too reserved. He only talked, drank and laughed, even when she had tried the massage to loosen him up and whispered in a sensual voice into his ears about how she wanted to use the restroom, “I'll be here waiting!” he said and he let her go by herself, the message would have been clear enough for some other guy. She had tried severally to loosen him up, yet nothing worked.

“I mean, yeah I'm good at conversations and you enjoyed that, but there are a lot other things that I'm equally good at.”

“Did you really mean what you said about me being boring?”

“Yes, the fact is, no women wants to be bored, women like spontaneous.”

“Spontaneous huh?”

“You said you had fun talking with me? Let me show you what real fun is like.”

His hands gripped hard at the steering as he felt her hands on him and suddenly she pulls out his dick as they drove on the express and slips it into her mouth. She pushed it all the way towards the back of her throats and it immediately stiffened.

“Whoa!” he freaked out, as he watched her in a matter of seconds he thought of ways to stop her, he had never experienced such spontaneous craziness in his life, and as he raised his eyes up to the roads, he quickly swerved the car from bumping into a stray dog and hit the brakes a little too late. The car went crashing into a huge tree by the forest along the quiet express road with a loud bang and all went silent. Smoke poured out of the car bonnet which was already crinkled. It was getting pitch dark when the police found their car in the accident scene and called for an ambulance.

Chapter 6

James woke up screaming "No, no, get off my dick!" he was half terrified. After a few seconds, he began to come out of his trance slowly, and realized that his kids were beside him, staring at him while he was lying on a hospital bed.

"Oh dad, you're awake!" Rachael hugged him passionately.

"What would we have done?" Richie said.

The hospital smelled of antiseptic cleaning agents and drugs, the smell made Richie's stomach roil but he didn't mind, his father had survived an accident and he basked in that knowledge.

James rubbed his temple, feeling a slight headache stir up as he sat up on the bed. He listened to his kid's emotional words and they kept going on and on about how life would have been hell without him, how lost they would feel, he began to replay the last scene before the accident in his head; this was an ugly reminder of Sarah, the girl who tried to give him a blow job while he was on the steering. He decided he would never see her again. Later on he sent a cheque to clear her hospital bills and a goodbye note attached to it. Luckily Sarah only sustained an arm injury and she was faring pretty well.

"Thank God it didn't turn out worse than this." James said.

"I'm so sorry I pushed you to Sarah, I feel like everything that happened was my fault."

"What happened?" James was astonished, he couldn't remember telling them exactly how they had had the accident and the screaming in his trance wasn't enough to let them know what had happened. He wouldn't have wanted all the dirty details spilled out.

"Oh my God, Did you lose your memory dad?" Sarah told us everything over the phone."

James felt like throwing up, *Goddamn Sarah, how the hell could she do that?* "She did? Well...I...I don't even remember what happened."

"We could fill you in with all the details-"

"Don't worry," he chipped in quickly, I don't like to rekindle bad memories."

Later on, James was discharged from the hospital and he returned home hale and hearty, although, not feeling quite ready to resume work so soon

"Ensure you get some rest." His children insisted.

"I think I'm trying too hard on women and it's not working." He said to his kids.

"Dad, don't give up on finding the right woman." Kevin said to him.

Tyler's call came in.

"Thank God you're alive. I'm pretty sure you've never considered writing a will." He said to James over the phone.

"Don't be so sure" James laughed. Later in the day, the staff showed up at his place with flowers and cards to wish him well. They spent a little time around his house, cracking jokes to make him laugh and make him feel special.

After a couple of days he began to walk with spring in his steps. He showed up at the office to check on the progress of their plan for the quarter and all was going smooth. Delilah's fashion sense had piqued since she got a huge paycheck. Carlos was excited to see him and asked for a selfie, but the other staff joined in the picture much to his disappointment.

"I'll be leaving you guys to continue with your work. I'm a bit tired and hungry."

James left the office and stopped over at a restaurant to eat. He had almost finished his plate of vegetable salad and chicken breast when he looked up at the lady sitting in front of him and something in him lit up. This one had an unusualness which he found interesting, she was not too young like the college girls; she was apparently not too heavily made up or wildly dressed like those he met over the internet. There was some classiness about her outlook and body language. She appeared like the perfect persona for his type of person; he immediately thought and couldn't take his eyes off her.

In the next minute, he was waiting for an opportunity to have her notice him, as soon as their eyes met, he smiled and waved at her. She smiled back and continued to eat. In the next few minutes, she was about to pick up her bag and leave when she heard a male voice in front of her.

"Hi, I'm James." She almost jumped.

"Melissa."

"Melissa, you're very gorgeous." He stated the obvious "But I know you get that a lot."

"Well, you're not wrong."

"So where are you headed."

"Back to work, we're having a meeting."

James offered to drop her at her office and asked her out on a dinner date.

"I'll be very busy, I'll have you know when I'll be free."

"Do have my contact then."

He was growing sick with anxiety expecting Melissa's call which didn't come; he had begun to think that perhaps she didn't have the same interest in him as he had in her.

One cool evening, his phone buzzed, he picked it up and the voice at the other end was calm and soothing.

“Melissa?”

“Yes, when would you be free? I’m having a flexible schedule.”

“I’m free now for dinner, what about you?”

“Ok, then.”

They arranged to meet at the same restaurant, Rich Table, at the hearts of San Francisco.

“Dad, where are you off to?” his kids asked almost in unison.

“For a dinner date...and yes, I like this one.”

He left them cheering behind.

The date went smoothly, he hadn’t overrated her, she was exactly the kind of woman he wanted in his life. She was knowledgeable about almost every aspect of life that mattered to him; they discussed business, sports, politics and entertainment. They talked about each other and it seemed as though they had no restraints in baring up their lives and even their past. They connected easily. Melissa was compassionate and down to earth. There were little peculiarities about her that he loved the most; the dimples that flashed naughtily on her cheeks whenever she smiled, the mischievous little snorting in her laughter, the way she smelled, the way she rolled her eyes in a conversation, and although she was a woman, there was a youthful girlishness about her, which James adored, and he thought anxiously that he couldn't wait for his kids to meet this one.

The second date they have was more like a picnic. Melissa wore a casual floral top and jeans with a flappy white hat and their picnic basket was stuffed with fruits.

"So you sit on the mat and nibble on these fruits."

James looked around uneasily,

"Scared there might be grasshoppers on the field?"

"Not really, I hardly go on picnic dates, I wonder if anyone I know could see me sitting on the grass like a kid."

Melissa laughed. "It's nothing. It's actually fun...look at those set of butterflies."

He watched a colourful throng go by "You know what? I have some of these in my belly sitting right next to you."

Mellissa looked into his eyes, probably not expecting his simplicity at that moment. They drew closer and kissed.

He got home that evening cheerful and glib, his kids noticed the changes. They had come to a point where they needn't bug him with questions about the new lady; they knew something was cooking and that he was going to let them in once he was ready. They at least felt satisfied for the first time.

The next time he was out on a date with Melissa, he noticed her reservation. She seemed to pick her words carefully, as though uncertain.

"Mellissa, you're my kind of woman and I would like to take this thing going on between us to the next level. I want a committed relationship with you."

Melissa circled the tip of her glass cup with a finger and didn't say much

"What is the matter, don't you like me the same way?"

"I do James, but I've committed in a relationship that ended up a disaster because the man had rigid dos and don'ts and it wasn't long before we figured out we weren't really each other's type. I'm just a little skeptical, I would like you to know every single bit of information about me and I just want to make sure you're my kind of man."

"Why, is there something about me that tells you I'm not?"

She hesitated and replied carefully "I like you James, but most of the time I am the one coming up with new stuffs for us to do or talk about. I'm leading the energy and it's a little masculine or perhaps, I'm pulling you into subtle pretenses."

"No, I'm totally fine with everything, I know I may be new to some things but I can adjust."

"Are you sure about this James, 'cause you seem a little rigid and unadventurous, I'm the one pulling your feet the whole time. It's a little unexciting to say the least."

Oh no, not again, he thought*, not those same words, rigid, unexciting, at least not from Melissa, he would do anything to not wear those labels when with her.*

"I really want to be perfect for you Melissa."

"You should date me without bending over backwards, and I wouldn't want you to be under any pressures at the same time."

"Oh, no, not at all, some things are just deep buried inside of us and it takes a little inspiration to lct it out."

Mellissa was smiling from ear to ear. She was at least glad that he's open to changes.

"Watch me show you a different version of myself. Hey, I could be really spontaneous. I'll take the lead this time around." James reassured.

Mellissa smiled again "You're really a nice person."

They had dinner and he dropped Melissa off at her doorstep and deciding to be a gentleman, he pecked her cheek and left for his house. Melissa thought that perhaps there was room for more, for him to check out her apartment and steal a deeper kiss and then she thought perhaps he didn't want to do the expected, perhaps it was all too cliché and he wanted to do this in a different style. Her thoughts trailed off into sleep.

James thought about Melissa all night and the following morning he found himself replaying their last conversation in his head. He felt a tinge of sadness each time he remembered the words Melissa had described him with, of all the times several people in his life had described him in that manner, this was the very first time he had ever felt bad about it. There certainly ought to be something he could do about it, he didn't want to be the stiff guy anymore. He remembered Sarah's words to him the day they had the car accident *"...the fact is, no woman wants to be bored, women like spontaneous."*

That morning, unable to get Melissa off his mind, an idea came to his mind, his mind circled around it and his eyes lit up. He was going to take the bull by the horns and do things that she will be excited about. He decided to play out the thoughts in his head thinking out loud to himself, how she's going to love what he's about to do. He brought out the new phone his kids had bought him, he remembered how impressive the camera picture were, he undressed himself, looked down on his dick which was semi erect and took a shot of it. His face flushed red, he couldn't believe what he was doing but he felt half excited and half nervous as he sent the picture to Melissa's phone. *She wants crazy, exciting, spontaneous, that's exactly who I'm gonna be from now onwards.* He was as anxious as someone who was performing a new art for the first time in a stage filled with important dignitaries.

As soon as he had sent the picture, he couldn't get his mind off it; he wondered if she had seen it, he wondered what looks would first appear on her face. He couldn't get his mind off the fact that this was the first time he was doing something as carefree as that. He was bent on winning Melissa's heart completely no matter what it took him. He began to have anxieties as he waited for her call and feedback. Thirty minutes went by and his phone hadn't buzzed, he wondered what Melissa might be doing at the moment. He picked up his phone and decided to call her.

"Hi Mellissa, how are you?"

"I'm doing fine, just having a really fast day. We have new clients to meet up with and we're trying to beat the time before some other organization gets ahead of us. You know how competitive some of these brands can be."

"I totally understand that tight situation, I hope you meet up."

"We're doing all we can." She smiled.

"Did you get my message?" He paused after his question, unable to hold his anxieties. He waited eagerly for her first reaction.

"Oh, no, I haven't checked my inbox. I'm actually on my way for the business meeting in Colombus Ohio conference centre, it's a very urgent one."

"Oh, I see."

"James...I really want to thank you for being in my life. You are a really nice person." James was smiling straight from his heart, he was pleased at the positive things she was saying about him, he grew warm. She continued to speak

"I like you very much because you're not like those crappy big guys who act all high and mighty and are quick to send their dick pics to ladies they just met and all that kind of stuff."

The smile went off James's face. He could feel a small heat rising in his chest and his cheeks flushing red. He couldn't believe what he had just heard. In the midst of his panic and fast throbbing heart, he realized that she was still speaking but he had become extremely uncomfortable

"So, I'll see you when I get back from the business trip. Goodbye." She said.

"Alright, bye" he forced himself to say.

And the call ended.

He still held the phone to his ears subconsciously, feeling more anxious and confused than he was before the call. He knew instantly that if she sees the picture message he had sent to her, it was all over between them. *What do I do?* He questioned himself and smashed a distraught fist into the air in frustration. *How on earth could I not have been able to tell that she wasn't that type, I'm such an idiot!*

He began to dial Tyler's number, in a few minutes Tyler's baritone voice came on the line

"Hello James."

"Tyler, I'm in deep shit right now, can I see you right now?"

Chapter 7

Minutes later, Tyler drove up to his apartment, wondering what could be wrong with his boss.

"James are you alright?" he said when he saw him looking devastated.

"Tyler, I'm in deep shit. I don't know what came over me and for the first time I decided to be naughty and adventurous with my new babe, and I...I sent her a picture of my dick."

"You fucking what? Oh my God, what a prestigious thing to do!" at the back of his mind he was glad it wasn't something that concerned the office.

"Don't start with the sarcasm."

"I mean, why in the world would you send a dick pic like a toddler James?" He slapped a hand on his forehead.

"You're making me feel worse, I'm sure that's not the worst thing you've ever heard a man do for love."

"Jesus! People in love buy flowers and candies. What were you thinking James?"

"I don't know....but stop being so judgmental."

"Don't you think you should extend the boundaries of my job to your heart matters, I think you need some serious guiding and counseling before you do the unthinkable once again and ruin your life this time around."

"Fine, what do I do? That's the important thing right now."

"First of all, what did she say when she saw it?"

"She hasn't seen it yet. She's in a business meeting, but very soon she's going to see it, the meeting wouldn't take forever I assume."

Tyler's face suddenly lit up. "I think you should stop her then before she sees it."

"How?"

"I don't know, just go get it; wherever the device is."

"She's travelled don't you get it?"

"Shit. To where?"

"Ohio, she said she'll be attending a meeting at the conference centre in Ohio."

"Do you know where that is?"

"Nope."

"Oh my God, this is a real mess."

“There’s Nationwide Hotel and conference centre in Ohio, which I know of, how do we make sure that’s the exact one?”

“I have no idea, she only mentioned Columbus Ohio.”

“Yes, that’s it, it’s in Columbus Ohio. I seem to remember the exact location now.”

“So how do we get there fast, she may as well be looking at the pic right now. We need to act fast just in case she’s stalling to check her message.”

“Let’s use your private jet.”

“Gosh this is so dumb.”

“What’s dumb is the idea of a billionaire sending his dick pic like a fucking teenage kid in the first place. Let’s get the hell out of here James.”

In the next few minutes they were on their way to board James’s private jet to Ohio. They got to the common hangar where a pilot was waiting for them and in the next minute they were airborne. Tyler fell asleep during the journey and James had to nudge him awake the moment they had landed.

“We’re here.”

“Hire a car. Call her up and give her a surprise.”

“Yeah and then do what?”

"Ask her for her phone or snatch it." Tyler said.

"This is not a joke Tyler. How do I even convince her that I need to look through her phone in the first place? What if she panics and doesn't hand it to me? As a matter of fact, what in the world am in doing in Ohio in the first place, so suddenly after we spoke? This has got to make sense Tyler else I'm screwed."

Tyler breathed out and looked into the air in deep thoughts and then a smile touched the corner of his lips. "I have an idea, please don't say no, this is the only way out."

"What?"

"Rob her."

"Christ, are you fucking kidding me, that's the silliest idea I've heard in a long while."

"Trust me James, that's the best idea at the moment. Get a frigging mask, tail her, kidnap her, I'll just rent a cab maybe, bring her to the location I'm going to arrange for us right now."

"I'm not doing that."

"We have to."

"Wouldn't she know I'm the one?"

"She wouldn't find out, unless of course you talk in the same voice. So you've got to use a falsetto voice, you're under a mask so she won't suspect a thing, besides, how on earth would you be in Ohio when she thinks you are in San Fransisco? You've got to get that phone only as a robber."

"Ok, I'm trying to get used to this idea gradually." He shut his eyes and inhaled as though trying to let it sink in.

"There's no time for getting used to the idea James, there's only time enough to act. Wait here, let me get a mask, hand gloves and perhaps a few other things."

Tyler hurriedly dashed off. James stood around waiting for him, trying not to weigh the whole situation in his head too much; he could feel the heavy throbbing of his heart and the sweat forming on his skin. He watched the cars pass by, he saw Mellissa in the looks of other women passing by and he knew it was just a fleeting fear of being suddenly bumped into by her.

The meeting at Ohio conference centre was full of drawn plans and ambitious targets by the participating organizations, the members were bursting with energy, Mellissa had become mentally exhausted as at the moment she left the conference room. Outside, the sun masked her with a renewing vigour as she hailed a cab approaching her.

"Take me to Short North, Mandrake Rooftop." she got in and sank unto the seat. The door at the other side pulled open immediately and shut, before she could let out a scream, a masked man clasped his hands over her mouth and the driver who was putting on dark sunshades took off.

“I’ve got a gun, don’t be rough, don’t fight it, and don’t try to be smart and I promise we won’t hurt you.”

“So what do you want from me?” she cried

“It’s just a little robbery that’s all.”

Her eyes dilated.

They drove through a quiet road in silence till they came to a peculiar, half-completed warehouse.

“Step out please.”

Mellissa shook. James felt compassionate for her, even though it wasn’t a real robbery, he felt himself slip into an emotional mess for putting her through the whole tension. She had looked into his eyes twice each time he spoke, his heart beat fast as he wondered if she could notice any familiarity in him or in his voice, even as he faked it.

When they had all come out, he said to her “You don’t have to fear a thing, we only want your phone, hand it over.”

Mellissa took out her phone and the driver stretched out his gloved hands and James could see that Melissa’s phone looked a little different from the one he knew, it in fact looked unfamiliar.

“Where is your phone?” there was an emphasis in his tone.

“What are you – how did you even know that I have another anyway?”

“Don’t fuck with us.”

“Fine, I gave it to my cousin.”

There was long silence, both silent and agonizing and he asked, “Which of your cousins, I mean, what’s her name?”

“Olivia.”

He took her phone and began to look through. “Olivia Creston?”

“Yes.”

He continued to look through the phone.

“She’s a beauty.” Tyler said.

“And where exactly is your cousin?”

“I don’t know.”

“Don’t fuck with us. Give us an address” Tyler said

Melissa thought that if he gave them the address to her work place, it would be more difficult for them to penetrate a big popular media house without making the news immediately.

“You really want to know? She’s in LPTV news channel, San Fransisco. Don’t get your ass caught trying to steal my iPhone for whatever reason, you guys don’t seem so professional to me anyways.”

James stifled a smile underneath his mask, “and how would you know that?”

"Where's your gun, I've been meaning to ask?"

James's heart skipped a beat "I told you earlier, it's under my waist."

"Well, I don't think you have a gun and I assure you i picked up a few karate skills, if you have no gun..."

James began to move backwards towards the car. Melissa cracked her knuckles and just then Tyler adjusted his mask and brought out a small black gun from his pocket.

"I'll shoot your smart ass bitch."

James nudged him "She's not a bitch."

"Shut up, you'll ruin this" he whispered.

Melissa watched them both uncertainly and raised both hands in the air.

Tyler quickly sent Olivia's picture to his phone and said "Lucky we didn't like your phone, you can keep it." he handed the phone back to her, and the two men turned back, walked a small distance towards their parked car and in the next minute they drove off with Melissa standing there shocked at what had just happened. She felt completely drained for the day. She suspected the men had parked a little distance away and walked into building so she couldn't see the car plate number. She had just thought of calling the cops but realized she had no vital information to give to them neither had she truly been robbed.

She thought of her endangered cousin and began to dial her number immediately.

***

"Did you hear how sexy that sounded, she knows karate! Who is she? I don't even know her!" James squealed as they sped through the streets.

"Do you even believe her? She's too sexy to know all that hard stuff."

"Apparently, there might be other things I don't know about her or perhaps she isn't even free to discuss with me, for reasons I may not know of."

"You have that aura, a lady wants to please you and keep off anything she thinks might displease you at all cost, that might be because she doesn't think you're open-minded enough to accept a lot of things. You know, big guys like you have some hard rules." Tyler said as he moved the steering.

"Are you tilting towards the same ugly point everyone has been making about me? Why is everyone bent on getting into my head?" James rolled his eyes.

"Come on, I'm your PA, who is in the best position to assess you so well? I don't think anyone is getting into your head James, calm down."

"You know what, I'm getting sick and tired of hearing it anyways, 'cause this is exactly how I got into this mess. I shouldn't have let anyone tell me how I should be. My authentic self wouldn't send a dick pic to a lady just to impress her."

"You're right, that was silly. I wouldn't do that."

James exhaled deeply.

"I'm sorry. I don't mean to keep judging."

Tyler drove quietly for some minutes and then he seemed to remember something "And by the way, you almost seemed unconvincing, that's why Mellissa wanted to turn the tables on you."

"Well, obviously, I'm not a thief... Now, what's the next move, how do we get to her cousin in LPTV? We need to get back to San Fransisco."

"What? You want to go rob the cousin?"

"Of course we have to, but guess what? I wouldn't be able to do this dirty job a second time, I'm a reputable billionaire under a thief mask just cause of a dick pic, I don't know what's weirder than that. So what we'll do is hire some thugs. Hey watch out don't beat the traffic!" James yelled.

"It's funny we're about to hire criminals to kidnap a lady and you worry about us breaking a traffic rule?"

"You are incorrigible Tyler."

Tyler laughed, “I know. So I assume Mellissa could be trying to get across to her cousin right now, to warn her and ask her to be at alert. We need to act fast.” Tyler reasoned.

“You’re right. Do you know how I can get across to these bad boys?”

Tyler smiled, parked their car and began to scroll through numbers on his phone. “I know just the men for this job. Oh shit, I’m getting a little too excited; I think I’m having a boner over this.” He looked at James whose face looked disapproving of his excitement.

“I’m sorry.” He muttered with a smile still lingering on his face.

In the next few minutes, James was on the phone with some group of thugs, making arrangements for the immediate kidnap of Olivia, Melissa’s cousin.

“Yeah, LPTV, so you can trail her from there...yeah...Tyler’s just forwarded her picture to you guys right away.”

“Yes, we’ve seen it...oh shit...she’s pretty hot.”

“Well, if you think so.”

“Is it just gonna be kidnap or can we rape her a little?”

“What the fuck, no rape please!” James was almost turning red.

“Just a little quickie?”

“No!”

“it’s not gonna be a full rape dude...how about just the tip goes in?”

“No! No rape, I insist.”

“Fine.” They sniggered mischievously at the background. James rolled his eyes “Horny asses. You can wank off her pic afterwards though, if you don’t mind...I’m coming over with my PA. Have the girl ready for us. I repeat, no rape, keep her as safe a newborn. We’ll be right there.”

They ended the call. In the next few minutes they were on a flight back to San Fransisco.

***

Olivia sat hands and feet bound on the chair in the empty room, the thugs had left her alone. She was drowning in her thoughts, imagining what the thugs wanted from her, if they had wanted cash they wouldn’t be wasting so much time. Her fears and anxieties continued to heighten the more she waited there. After about thirty minutes, the door creaked open and a masked man walked in. she swallowed frightfully, her heart thumping wildly.

“Olivia, you really look pretty as they say, almost as pretty as your cousin. Has she called you today?” James asked.

Olivia was silent, as though picking the safest possible answer to give to the masked man with a strange voice which sounded obviously altered.

“Don’t lie to me.” He added.

"I did miss her calls, so yes, she tried to reach me but we haven't spoken. I wanted to call her back when I get out of the office because I was on air, but as soon as I left the office I got accosted by some thugs who shoved me into their car and drove off as though they've been waiting for me and then, here I am."

"Well then, you have nothing to worry about, just hand me your phone and we'll be over and done with this. I'm aware there's a phone your cousin gave to you and another which belonged to you ever since, I want the former."

"That's gonna be a problem sir."

"Why?"

"My cousin, Mellissa, gave me her phone because mine fell into the lake we went fishing and picnicking at reeky lake, but unfortunately the one she had just given to me got stolen by one of the thugs who had just kidnapped me."

Chapter 8

“What?” James’s face drained of color. He couldn’t believe what he had just heard from Olivia, the thugs had stolen her phone; the very phone he had brought her here to get out of her. His head spun as Olivia continue to speak.

“Yes, one of them kept on talking about how my ass was perfect, how he would have loved to rape me, but since he can’t get that from me, he needs to take something else and then he took the phone.”

“Oh my god. Stupid idiots!” James yelled, “Well...It’s alright, like I said...” he figured that he had let go of his falsetto voice subconsciously and quickly switched up “Like I said, you have nothing to worry about, I’m not here to harm you. I’ll have you released in a jiffy and you’ll act like nothing had happened, do you understand?”

She nodded a little.

Mellissa’s call came to his phone, “excuse me” he said and left to answer it.

“Hi Mellissa, are you alright? You sound uneasy.” He hated himself for saying that.

"I got into a bit of trouble to say the least."

"What trouble?"

She narrated her experience with the two guys who had attempted to robe her of her phone. He feigned shock and hated himself instantly for it. He began to console and pacify her.

"No one is ever going to harm you darling. I know you're quite careful too but shit happens, try not to think about it. I'm glad they didn't hurt you."

He spoke for another five minutes and by the time he dropped the call, he found that he was missing her a lot. Olivia got released immediately and James began to dial Stony's number, the leader of the gang that had arrested her.

"Dude, where's her phone? You stupid fuck, that's why I wanted her in the first place!"

"Oh, I didn't know that, you held out on us. How the fuck were we supposed to know we were doing all these because of a goddamn phone?"

"I didn't hold out on you, goddamn it, I just didn't think it was necessary to ask you not to steal her phone because I wanted it."

"You only asked not to rape. Ok...fine...so how do you want the phone delivered?"

"In person please."

"You don't get it do you? You would have to pay a good sum of money for the phone."

"Stony, I already paid you for the services."

"This is business James. This is a fresh lead for us and a new treasure is at stake."

James's shoulders sank as he breathed out deeply, feeling exasperated already.

"And how much are you talking about?"

"fifty thousand dollars maybe"

"Are you out of your fucking mind?" James screamed, "Do you have any idea you're talking about just a fucking phone?"

"You're up to it dude. You sound pretty interested in this little phone and I don't care to know why and you don't want me to go digging cause it might make the price a little higher than what I propose. "

"I'll never have anything to do with you after this."

"That's right good fella, you're obviously not the telephone-some-thugs type of guy and we can tell. But if you need this last deal straight just pay up and get your phone."

James thought of everything he had at stake, he didn't trust the thugs neither was he sure what they were capable of, they could even set him up with the police. He decided quickly and sent over a cheque and in the next two hours the phone was delivered to him by a young teenage boy with a friendly smile which he had never met before. James felt once again as though his life is back in order. He checked through the phone and deleted the file he had sent. All that trouble just for a single dick pic, he thought sheepishly and exhaled, finally the panic was all over. There was a renewed spark of energy in him, he was glad to have a second chance to right his wrongs and make Melissa's fall head over heels in love with him.

Yoga came to his mind, he thought of all the renewed energy and positivity he could get from an hour of yoga and other exercise and he got down to it. after an hour and thirty minutes he lay down on the ground as his phone rang, he was so tired, it had almost rang out before he got up and picked it.

"Hello"

A familiar voice spoke at the end of the other line.

"Who's this?"

"We just finished a deal."

"Stony? What the hell are you calling me for?"

"Relax, let's have a little chitchat-"

"Look I've got no time to waste on chitchats" James interrupted impatiently

“Listen, I want to know, why exactly did you want that phone so badly?”

“What the fuck, that’s none of your business dude!”

“It actually is, it’s our business. Well, I saw the damn file.”

“What are you talking about?” his voice was laced with a shiver of panic.

“I’m not a novice James, we’ve seen a lot on this line of business. What amazes me is that it wasn’t even a picture but a video, the idiot in the video thought he was taking a picture and ended up making a short video of his body. Who else would do a silly thing as that if not you James?”

“Oh my God! Fuck me!” James exclaimed “I should have taken a look at that, well, thank God it’s delete”

A hollow laugh vibrated into his ears from the other line “You are so hilarious? You deleted it huh? Well how about this, what if I told you that I have your short funky sexy clip and I just realized that I haven’t charged you for the actual worth of what you want.

“Fuck you Stony!”

He laughed out again. James’s face flushed red, he could feel the throbbing on his temples, he felt like exploding.

“This is cheap blackmail.”

“You’re right and wrong at the same time. It’s blackmail, but this isn’t going to be cheap James. Do you have a few thousand dollars to get this clip non-existent or would you rather have your entire reputation in the line. You know what I can do James.”

“Why are you doing this to me?”

“No hard feelings James, you’re a business man I reckon, and this is just business.”

“Well, I’ll speak to my Personal Assistant and I’ll get back to you.”

“Hurry up, there’s so much on the line, you’re pretty big by the way.”

“Shut the fuck up!” James said and ended the call panting. He banged his fist on a table angrily and screamed incoherently. Just when he thought the troubles were all over, it seemed like it had just begun. His mind was spinning, he was thinking of many ways he could get out of this but he couldn’t figure any, surely Tyler would have a great idea, he thought. Paying another dime to them seemed too much of a rip off and what he was asking for was enormous. He had paid too dearly working with them in the first place, he wished it was all a story he could rewrite from the beginning so he would cut out the very part he conceived the idea of sending his nudes to Mellissa. He called Tyler on the phone and told him about the blackmail. Tyler tried not to sound exasperated, it was a part of his professionalism, but it was also because he felt like he had played a greater role in exposing his boss James to these thugs who have ended up being more trouble than a solution at the moment.

"I give up James, we have to use the cops."

"The cops? Are you sure this is going to work out? I really don't want my reputation further tarnished."

"Calm down and trust me James,"

"Trusting you has gotten me into further mess Tyler, I mean, how the hell did you ever come across these guys. If I didn't know you well enough, I'd think you were in on it."

"That's a little too forward and crazy; you can't go about trusting the bad people and suspecting the good people."

"Ok, the cops, do you think they can really handle this without keeping records about it or having to further expose the situation to the knowledge of more people?"

"They can handle this very easily and just the way you might want it, but you've got to let them into every bit of the details and let them know you want the file gone with the wind...you know what I mean."

"Are you suggesting any-"

"I'm glad we've worked so closely enough that you could read my mind boss."

"I've spent so much on this already."

"Just a small tipping and this could be the last. Trust me. I've got to go for an eye test; it seems I'm having troubles working lately with my eye condition."

"Sure Tyler. I was going to suggest that the other day."

Stony watched the clip over and over again till he was gradually getting hard. He felt smart that he had quickly figured out why James wanted the phone so badly but it had rather been out of his sexual interest than his smartness.

He was a macho homosexual man with a rugged face and a long scar running across his sunken cheek who liked to dominate his men in bed. The moment he had seen the video clip, he watched it with a knowing smile on his face and a keen interest in his loins.

He had shut the door that day and watched the short clip over and over till he subconsciously slipped his hands into his boxers and jerked his hard cock in a hard grip the way he liked it and in two minutes his boxers was slick with a full load of his cum.

Feeling satisfied, he washed his hands and in the next minute he dialed James's number to get down to business but the call hadn't been concluded on. His client-turned-victim said he was going to talk to his Personal Assistant and get back to him. Stony thought how so naïve and gentle James was and he began to grow hard again, he thought about how James would have made a good submissive had he been his gay partner. He imagined his cock moving through James's tight butthole and he could feel the hot throbbing of his cock immediately. Perhaps it was because he was daydreaming that he didn't quite hear the first voice of the cops ordering him to open the door or else they would break in. he hesitated, a stir of panic began to grow in him because he was a jail bird who had a list of crime he was suspected to have committed, he wasn't ready for them yet.

"Shit!" he muttered, got up from his seat and moved towards the window, at that point the door broke open and the cops yelled his name, it sounded distant and unfamiliar to him. Everyone called him stony but they called him Matt. He jumped on the window, staggered back and fell. He got up and made another attempt but the grip on his shirt was hard and almost ripped the flannel off his body. He fell back and crashed on the floor. Two of the policemen stood over him, and the third policeman began to search his apartment with their search warrant. He pushed hard against the other two men who held him back. "If you like it the hard way we'll have you rough handled Matt." He glared at them angrily as he stopped fighting, breathing hard.

They got a hold of his devices and found several nude clips on his phone, not sure which was which, the cops smashed the phone to pieces.

"Is that all?" a cop asked the other "So far, that's all he's got."

“Matt, we’ve got our eyes on you and the boys, I’m sure you know that already. We don’t want to add cheap blackmail for the things you’re going to be wanted for. Be a good boy.”

Stony panted hard from the panic and tussle with the cops. He knew he had no choice, he had lost the precious file in his possession to bits and he wasn’t going to make an extra dime like he had wanted. He exhaled. “Game over” he muttered feeling defeated, and as the cops walked away he thought everything had been all so stupid after all, a broad smile spread across his face.

James and Tyler breathed a sigh of relief after they got the good news from the cops. The device which stored the file had been smashed to smithereens and he was safe again. Best of all, Mellissa had gotten over the incident with the marauders and she was back in constant communication with James. It was like having a point of closure in his life that felt just as important as his other huge achievements.

He sat for a drink with Tyler, discussing recent events, laughing over it and picking subtle lessons from each.

“On a scale of one to ten James, how much do you think Mellissa likes you?”

“To be honest, these days we’ve drawn a lot closer after recent events so I’m giving it nine maybe.” He puffed his shoulders proudly.

“Well, that’s not bad at all, as we put a tick on your love life, we need to put a tick on your adeptness to using new devices. You do need to learn how to use these new phones don't you think, the world's leaving you behind."

They drank and laughed through their chitchat while discussing how much work there is to be done at the office tomorrow morning after the end of month meeting. I'll be a little late tomorrow James; I have to get my eye test result.

"Alright then."

As Tyler made his way across the room, James said "Hey Tyler, you're due for a little raise."

Tyler was taken by surprise, "Thanks James" he grinned and James nodded feeling grateful too.

Chapter 9

Perhaps, it was still the sudden peace that came with James's ended troubles that made him oversleep the morning and get up late. Remembering that he was supposed to lead the end of the month meeting as usual, he jumped out of bed and hurriedly began getting ready. He left the house in the nick of time and maneuvered through the heavy traffic.

He parked his white SUV and rushed straight to the meeting room. There was a strange feeling shrouding him, it was a little unusual, not because he was late or had kept them waiting, it was just the same odd feeling he had gotten the day he arrived home and sensed that the air was unusual before realizing his kids had thrown a wild party, this time around, it was all silent, yet, there had been an inexplicable foreboding in the air.

As he got to the entrance, he heard the unmistakable sniggering of his staff and little talks in the air, but what made him grow a little curious was that loud and clear, Carlos was playfully making a show for everyone to entertain them, or perhaps he now sounded so much like him it had become uncanny.

As soon as he walked in, his eyes were transfixed on the large projector where the voice was coming from and it wasn't Carlos's voice but his, and his eyes met with the clip they were watching and it was of him. The short clip of his nude display was being played over and over and jeered at. He turned instantly red; in the video he was stark naked as he proudly displayed his cock and did some raunchy talk as he recorded. The dick pic which had turned out to be a recording had found its way into their hands and as it played he saw glaringly the logo of a popular internet news channel at the top left corner – it had been in the news! His heart raced out of control.

"It's definitely him, no shit" Delilah said.

"His face isn't showing but the body size and voice is unmistakable" said Reeves

"If Tyler was here, he could have given us some background explanation..." Fred said

"God, he's huge!" Nicky

"Don't even think about that Nicky" Reeves warned.

They saw him standing by the door and the room became as silent as a graveyard. He looked at the big screen, it was his first time of watching the mess he had created, the very menace in his life lately – how on earth did it get here? He wondered with his head almost spinning on his neck. His heart throbbed mercilessly.

He walked into the room quietly, the video clip was playing on loop, eyes darted around each other, Fred signaled for the video to be turned off immediately but it was too late. At that point too, Tyler walked in, he looked at the big screen and saw the looks on everyone's faces and the shock in his eyes was glaring. The voice on the big screen was dirty talking and he remembered everything he had said on the day he tried to take the picture while it recorded him instead, it blared loud and clear:

"She's gonna love this dick pic...Oh god, I'm really doing this...Well, here goes daddy's dick...I bet she's gonna wet her victoria's secret." James almost walked out in shame, he wished he could vanish from the room instantly but he knew better, he needed to take responsibility of his actions. He would quickly address the situation although he had no explanation for it.

"Good morning everyone. James began, he so badly wanted to say something but he was short of words, he paused, trying to calm his mind so that he could at least find words. He looked up at Tyler and saw the shocked, questioning looks in his eyes and knew that he could feel a great portion of what he felt at the moment.

Carlos's voice interrupted the silence, "I am so sorry sir! Please don't fire me. I was trying to impress my girlfriend and I thought I'd do this video. I didn't know it would go this far."

Murmurings erupted.

"Oh my God, I sort of knew it."

“That makes a lot of sense, James wouldn’t do this.”

“Damn Carlos, I never knew he was bisexual.”

Carlos continued to speak “I’m really ashamed to have the entire staff watch this. I know it’s really an unethical behaviour and I tender my sincere apologies.” Carlos bowed his head. James was amazed; Carlos was the best actor he had ever seen. He couldn’t believe what was happening, he had just taken blame for the clip just to cover up his mess, and it was damn believable due to the similarity of their physique and voice. He was glad he hadn’t showed his face in the recording after all. He felt as though boulders had been lifted off his shoulders.

“Carlos, we’ll talk about this...incompetence and...” it was as though he forced the words out of his throat “this unethical behaviour later.” The meeting has been adjourned till after lunch break. Now, you all get to work.”

Tyler smiled. As they all walked out of the meeting room in a single file, Carlos heard James’s voice call out “Hey Carlos, stay behind.”

As soon as it was just James and Carlos at the meeting room, he said to him with a broad grin on his face.

“You just got a raise.”

“Thank you Sir. I’m super excited.”

“No, thank you.” James slapped Carlos’s butt on his way out of the door, it was a memorable moment for him as he headed out of the door, his body tingling with excitement and an emotional smile on his face – that was a butt slap he would cherish for the rest of his life.

Chapter 10

Even though James had been on several dates with Melissa, he eagerly looked forward to this one; so many things were running through his mind as they were on Melissa's. He felt like he hadn't seen her for years and meeting with her in the beautiful Rich Table restaurant, where they had first met was quite significant.

He arrived there first, he sat taking a drink, wondering all the emotions he would feel when he saw her again, he was sure that amongst the excitement would be guilt for all the things he had done to salvage his mess. His drink was half empty when Melissa walked in, for a moment the world became still, the air was filled with her fragrance, his heart raced, and he could feel his cheeks flush. She made him feel like some college kid in love for the first time and he knew instantly that she had been worth all that trouble.

As she sat, he took her hand and kissed it "You look lovelier than ever."

"And there's a fresh energy in that haircut and the weight of your voice, you sure must have had a terrific weekend."

"Well, it turned out terrific. I wouldn't say it was all smooth though."

The waiter took her order and they ate and talked casually. Melissa blushed each time he looked deep into her eyes. He was wiping the corners of his mouth when Melissa said "You're pretty huge"

He thought he heard Mellissa say something that sounded like it but he was probably just having an auditory hallucination from a subtle trauma stemming from recent events.

"What?"

"I said you're pretty huge." She winked at him. His tongue went dry. *Jesus Christ, she had watched the goddamn clip!*

"...and I like the kinky talk too" she said and crinkled her nose a bit.

"Oh – my – God. How on earth...This must have really gone viral." James flushed red and an unexpected laughter busted out of him.

"It's kinky, perhaps because I know you're clearly not that type and it would take anyone by surprise, it makes it a lot more interesting so i perceived it differently and I was able to make sense out of recent events that had left me curious to say the least. It shows you are capable of a lot more things than I thought James, that's the flexibility and spontaneity I've always desired. You're every woman's dream – smart, decent, spontaneous, funny, reliable, rich, and crazy. Every little spice is all embedded deep within you."

A couple sitting right beside them had been watching with smiles on their faces, James didn't know for how long they had been there observing. A creepy thought came to his mind; what if more people than he thought recognized him? What if they had all watched the video? He began to grow a little anxious but the fact that Melissa who was more important than any other viewer as far as he knew, had just complimented it and made it seem a lot lighter incident than he had thought it, gave him a sense of calm, he seemed a lot reassured.

He couldn't believe he had gone through that whole trouble for nothing. He was at the peak of his emotions that moment and he said to her "oh, you like crazy huh? I got one more crazy for you." He knelt down on the cold marble of the exquisite restaurant and said to Melissa "Would you marry me?"

Melissa's face straightened, that entire smile vanished into what looked like disbelief and then the smiled returned back with an outburst of joy "Yes, Yes James" and she threw his arms around him. She looked at his hands expectantly and he quickly chipped in "I'm sorry, this couldn't wait till there was a ring shopping so I have no-"

"Here's our ring, it's for sale buddy!" interrupted the goofy couple who had been watching them excitedly, and half in tears. James looked at them and found that they were offering the gold traditional ring on the wife's finger for sale. "How much would you resell it?"

"Ten thousand dollars!"

"What! It's way overpriced but anyway...no one sells a used ring for that amount! James looked over to Mellissa who was smiling and looking the other way, trying not to get involved in the awkward transaction. fine, I'll pay you bunch of highway robbers. He got out his little cheque book and signed him a cheque at the spot. Very quickly she took it off her finger and Melissa laughed though the whole drama, James took the pretty ring and said to Melissa "Now here." There was screaming, laughter and applaud before James realized that a small crowd had formed at the restaurant spot, watching them. Still on his knee, he slipped the ring on her finger and it seemed loose, apparently it wasn't her size.

In unison the teary couple screamed "No refunds!"

The entire restaurant applauds making noises of excitement as the newest couple kissed.

An idea quickly struck James, he took out his new phone and snapped a picture of Melissa's ring on her finger and forwarded a message to multiple contacts which included his children, close friends, Tyler and his other staff, and captioned it; *James engages Mellissa, engagement dinner party at Rich Table restaurant.*

Tyler replied with a text message immediately: *Beautiful...not the ring, but the picture successfully taken and sent, you nailed it this time. He ended with laughter emojis.*

James smiled. His phone immediately rang and it was his daughter, Rachel. She was so garrulous over the phone in her excitement. "Daddy, we're organizing a proper engagement party for you guys right here."

"Oh no, you don't have to go through all that stress"

"Daddy, this is what we're good at, our college frat and reunion party was lit wasn't it dad?"

"Well...err..."

"You know we're good at this. Let's make one of the best moments of your life well celebrated."

"I'm really happy Rachael...and you know the best part. The best moments of my life will be every day when Melissa becomes my wife."

"I believe so dad."

The engagement party turned out amazing; there was a rock band, special delicacies from the best city chefs, decoration in a grand style, bottles of champagne, expensive gifts and souvenirs.

James had so much acknowledging to do at the party, first, he acknowledged Tyler for his steadfast friendship and acumen in running his business and personal life, even though his ideas may not be perfect. He also thanked his entire staff for their hard work and his children for their support and then he made a full toast to Melissa who had become everything he had wished for.

He announced the looming of a new branch for JC corporations and that the old branch will be managed by Tyler. He announced a promotion for his entire staff and an upcoming recruitment. "Let's talk more about Mellissa and James." Tyler interrupted his chain of announcements. "Yes, you're almost always right Tyler. Today is for us, the newest couple." Finally, James and Melissa fixed a grand wedding slated for the following month and it would be covered by the top media in San Francisco.

Melissa felt as though her entire life had changed for the better, the affluence she had become a part of, was to a level she never dreamt possible and for James, it felt too as though his life had changed for the better but it was more than that for him, getting married to Melissa, he felt, was a dream come true.

Want more books from Brian Obodeze?

SCAN THE QR CODE
TO SEE OTHER
AWESOME BOOKS FROM THE AUTHOR

www.ingramcontent.com/pod-product-compliance
Lightning Source LLC
LaVergne TN
LVHW050323160826
845677LV00014B/3523
* 9 7 9 8 8 4 8 8 0 5 0 1 7 *